It's the Easter Beagle, Charlie Brown

 LITTLE SIMON

An imprint of Simon & Schuster Children's Publishing Division
1230 Avenue of the Americas, New York, New York 10020

Adapted from the works of Charles M. Schulz

It's the Easter Beagle, Charlie Brown™

By Charles M. Schulz
Adapted by Justine and Ron Fontes
Illustrated by Paige Braddock
Based on the television special produced by
Lee Mendelson and Bill Melendez

LITTLE SIMON
New York   London   Toronto   Sydney   Singapore

The winter snow had melted. Flowers were in bloom. The entire Peanuts gang was getting ready for Easter!

Peppermint Patty was teaching her friend Marcie how to decorate Easter eggs.

"I got the eggs, sir, just like you asked," Marcie said.

"You get the eggs ready, and I'll mix up all the colors," Peppermint Patty said. "And please stop calling me sir!"

While Peppermint Patty was busy with the dyes, Marcie cooked the eggs. "All the eggs are fried, sir. Now, how do we color them?" she asked.

Peppermint Patty and Marcie weren't the only ones with Easter problems. Sally didn't see how she could celebrate without new shoes.

Linus and Lucy needed eggs, baskets, and candy. "Want to go to the store with us, Sally?" Lucy asked.

"I told you, it's a waste of time," Linus said. "The Easter Beagle takes care of all that."

"Linus, you drive me crazy!" Lucy cried.

But Sally was curious. "Who's the Easter Beagle?" she asked.

"Sally," Linus explained, "we don't need to go to all this trouble. On Easter Sunday the Easter Beagle comes dancing along, passing out colored eggs to all the good little kids."

Charlie Brown sighed. His sister had been fooled before by Linus's holiday heroes. "Come on, Sally, I thought you wanted to get some new shoes."

At the store Charlie Brown, Sally, Linus, Lucy, and Snoopy met Peppermint Patty and Marcie.

"Hi, Chuck! What are you up to? We're here to get some eggs to color for Easter," Peppermint Patty said. "Marcie here fried the last batch." Then she whispered, "This kid doesn't quite get it, Chuck."

"It's a waste of time to buy and color eggs," Linus said, "because the Easter Beagle will do all that."

Peppermint Patty rolled her eyes. "Boy, Chuck, you sure have some strange friends. But c'mon, let's go buy some eggs. Easter Beagle, indeed!"

Sally found a pair of blue, high-heeled shoes. She couldn't walk in them, but they sure were different!

Snoopy found a hollow Easter egg. He looked inside and saw bunnies dancing.

Snoopy imagined dancing with the bunnies. His feet felt as light as flower petals, and his heart was full of Easter joy! The bunnies applauded his happy dance.

Linus kept trying to convince his friends to believe in the Easter Beagle.

Lucy lost her patience. "Good grief! There's no Easter Beagle!" she declared.

Sally wanted to believe Linus, but she had been disappointed before. "This sounds faintly familiar. I remember sitting in a stupid pumpkin patch all night waiting for the Great Pumpkin."

"This is different," Linus explained. "That was Halloween. This is Easter. The Easter Beagle will *never* let you down," he insisted.

"Well," said Sally slowly, "I really want to believe you, because I like you. But I just don't know."

Marcie and Peppermint Patty brought their freshly bought eggs back to Peppermint Patty's kitchen. This time Marcie was sure she was cooking the eggs right. She put some in the waffle iron! Then she tried to put one in the toaster! When that didn't work, Marcie used the oven.

AARGH!

Once again Marcie had ruined all the eggs! Peppermint Patty's sandals slapped the sidewalk as she stomped back to the store. At this rate, they'd finish making Easter eggs in July!

On the way they met Linus.

"Hi! Where are you going in such a hurry?" Linus asked.

"We keep running out of eggs," Peppermint Patty complained. "I'm still trying to show Marcie how to color eggs for Easter Sunday."

"You're making a mistake," Linus reminded them. "On Easter Sunday the Easter Beagle brings eggs to all the good little children."

"Sir, is this right?" Marcie asked. "Perhaps we don't have to go to all this trouble. If this Easter Beagle—"

Peppermint Patty sighed. "Kid, I'm having enough problems without your crazy stories. C'mon, Marcie, let's get another dozen."

"It's a waste of time!" Linus called after them.

When they got back to the kitchen Peppermint Patty told Marcie exactly how to cook the eggs. "These eggs are not to be fried, roasted, toasted, or waffled. These eggs must be boiled."

Marcie filled a pot with water and turned on the flame.

"Put the eggs in now. When the water comes to a boil let me know," Peppermint Patty said.

Marcie cracked the eggs into the pot one by one. "Okay, sir, all the eggs are in."
"Good, Marcie. Let them boil a long time. Then I'll show you how to paint them," Peppermint Patty told her.

After awhile Marcie said, "The eggs look done, sir."

On the way to the stove Peppermint Patty sniffed the air. "That's funny. It smells like soup," she said.

Peppermint Patty looked into the pot and cried, "You made egg soup! Arrrgh!"

Peppermint Patty didn't know what to do, so she complained to her friends. "We don't have enough money for more eggs. How can I teach Marcie about Easter?"

Once again Linus reminded the gang: "Don't worry. The Easter Beagle will bring eggs to all the good little kids, and everyone will be filled with great joy."

Peppermint Patty sighed. "Kid, I hope you're right." Her egg-dyeing days were over!

No matter what Linus said, Lucy wasn't counting on the Easter Beagle. She made her very own Easter eggs for her own Easter egg hunt.

"You're wasting your time," Linus cried.

"Leave me alone!" Lucy said. "Don't bother me with your stupid ideas." She had a practical Easter plan that was guaranteed to work. "Easter is very simple," she explained. "You paint the eggs. You hide the eggs. You find the eggs. And you know who's going to find them? Me! Because I'm the one who's going to *hide* them."

When all her eggs were colored, Lucy put them in a big basket and took them to the field where the Easter celebration would take place. Each time she hid an egg, she wrote down where she put it.

Lucy couldn't wait for Easter Sunday. She was going to have the greatest Easter egg hunt ever!

On Easter morning Peppermint Patty and Marcie went to the field for their big party. Peppermint Patty apologized to her friend. "I'm sorry we don't have any Easter eggs, Marcie."

"I'm the one who's sorry, sir," Marcie replied. "I guess I'm not much of a cook."

Peppermint Patty sighed. "I've seen this happen on holidays before. You look forward to being really happy. Then something happens that spoils it all."

Charlie Brown knew just what Peppermint Patty meant. To him, every holiday was just another day to be disappointed. "I know why they have holidays: so people can get together and have fun," Charlie Brown sighed. "So why am I alone?"

Sally was also unhappy. She scolded Linus. "I've been waiting for the Easter Beagle since dawn. Where is he?!" She had that pumpkin-patch feeling all over again.

"Why do I listen to you? 'Trust me,' you said. Now I've been burned again. Never trust a man with a blanket," she fumed. "Get me my lawyer!"

Suddenly the Easter Beagle danced into view in the field behind Linus and Lucy's house! Over his arm he carried a bright basket brimming with colorful eggs. His feet were as light as flower petals. His smile was pure joy!

"The Easter Beagle is coming!" Linus cried with delight.
All the children stared in amazement at this wonderful vision of spring!

The Easter Beagle tossed eggs to Peppermint Patty, Marcie, Linus, and Sally. "Thank you, Easter Beagle!" Linus cried.

The Easter Beagle gave eggs to Schroeder and Lucy. He even tossed an egg into Woodstock's birdhouse. And wherever his dancing feet touched the ground, joy sprang up like daffodils on the first day of spring.

But by the time he reached Charlie Brown the Easter Beagle's basket was empty.

Charlie Brown sighed. Of course he wouldn't get anything. He never did. Nothing but rocks on Halloween, no cards on Valentine's Day, and now no eggs on Easter. No matter what day it was, he was still Charlie Brown.

"What do we do with our Easter eggs now that we have them, sir?" Marcie wondered.

"Put a little salt on them and eat them," Peppermint Patty replied.

Marcie salted her egg then bit into it, shell and all. *CRUNCH!* "Tastes terrible, sir."

Peppermint Patty could not believe her sweet, clueless friend. Marcie was lovable, but she just didn't get it!

"See, Linus was right. There *is* an Easter Beagle," Sally said.

Lucy looked at the striped egg that Snoopy had given her. It looked very familiar. "Some Easter Beagle," she scoffed. "He gave me my own egg!"

Lucy was furious! She had painted and hidden those eggs, and *she* was supposed to find them all!

"Why don't you go talk to the Easter Beagle?" Linus suggested.

Lucy decided to confront Snoopy at his doghouse. "Put up your dukes!" she cried.
  Lucy was ready for a fight. Instead, Snoopy popped out of his doghouse and kissed her!
Suddenly Lucy felt all the giddy joy of spring. For once Linus was right about something. Easter mean
flowers, fun, and most of all . . . the Easter Beagle!